B53 105 270 2

KU-862-795

Op

agull

was

red

he

a

A book for Florence

BS3 IOS 270 2

ISBN 978-0-9930976-0-7

First Printing, 2014
Published by Ruth Cooper

Printed in the United Kingdom

RUTH COOPER

Sloop
the Seagull
who was
Scared
of the
Sea

Illustrated by JULIE CHAMBERS

Published by Ruth Cooper

Sloop perched on the cliff top with the sea breeze ruffling his feathers. He looked at his classmates flying happily over the sea.

Gliding and diving, the other gulls had fun every playtime. Sloop was sad, he wanted to join in but was too scared to fly over the water.

"Come on Sloop," said his teacher, Mrs Gully, as she landed beside him. "You can't just watch all the time. Now back to class for the next lesson."

Sloop thought about what Mrs Gully had said. "I wish one day I will be brave enough to fly over the sea and maybe even as far as Lighthouse Island."

Then Saturday came.

Saturday was always fun, there was no school and the beach would get very busy.

There was always a lot to look at. Families would swim, snorkel and surf. They would build sand castles and fly kites.

Sloop played too with his best friend Breeze. Although, as usual, all their games were on land because Sloop was scared of the sea.

As Sloop and Breeze played the sky grew dark. Suddenly all the people on the beach picked up their towels, picnic baskets and toys. They began to leave the beach to go back to their cars, hotels and campsites.

"What is happening?" Sloop asked Breeze
nervously.

"It's only a thunderstorm and it will be
hours before it gets here," replied Breeze
knowingly.

Sloop looked at the waves getting bigger
and then looked up at the dark clouds
blocking the sun.

Sloop thought about leaving but Breeze insisted they play another game. "Time me flying over to Lighthouse Island!" Breeze asked excitedly, handing Sloop her stopwatch.

Breeze stood on the very edge of the cliff and flapped her wings in preparation. Sloop placed his wing on the big green start button. "Ready... Steady... Go!" shouted Sloop in his loudest squawk.

Ten, twenty, thirty... Breeze vanished into the dark clouds. Sloop began to panic. He felt big, cold drops of rain landing on him followed by a ROAR of thunder!

Sloop decided he needed to find help, quickly!

He flew to the beach shack looking for a grown up but it was shut. Apart from the younger seagulls from school he couldn't see anyone around, so he swooped over the roof top.

There he found Mrs Gully and Mr Squawk eating scraps of fish and chips.

"Mrs Gully, Mrs Gully! Mr Squawk, Mr Squawk!" Sloop was so frantic and was out of breath.

"What is it boy?" Mr Squawk asked abruptly. Mr Squawk didn't like being interrupted, especially when eating his dinner.

"It's Breeze... she has gone missing flying to Lighthouse Island. Please help me, please!" Sloop cried.

Mrs Gully and Mr Squawk leapt up.

Mr Squawk flew off to find Breeze's mum and dad whilst Mrs Gully stayed with Sloop. She told him something she knew Sloop really wouldn't want to hear...

To find Breeze they would have to fly over to Lighthouse Island! Of course Mrs Gully could have flown over on her own but only Sloop knew where Breeze was when she vanished.

Sloop gulped and felt his heart beat faster.

"I'll be with you all the way Sloop. Be brave," Mrs Gully said gently.

Sloop held his head up high and shuffled his feet, he flapped his wings and looked up at Mrs Gully. Together they took off into the air.

They flew over the beach shack and over the beach. Suddenly they were above the sea. As they flew it got deeper and deeper. The waves were very choppy, bouncing up and down.

Sloop and Mrs Gully flew into the dark cloud. They still couldn't find Breeze so they carried on flying.

At last they arrived at Lighthouse Island.

Sloop and Mrs Gully were soaked. Rain was dripping from their feathers and beaks. Mrs Gully shook her feathers dry but Sloop just stood there. He was dazed.

"I did it. I did it! I flew over the sea!" Sloop murmured.

The lighthouse flashed lighting up the land and sea in front of them. They looked for Breeze but still couldn't find her.

Mrs Gully had a good idea. If they went inside the lighthouse and climbed to the lookout at the top, they would be able to see for miles in ALL directions.

They snuck past Lighthouse Keeper Kip.

"Where are my sardines?" grumbled Kip very annoyed.

Sloop and Mrs Gully hopped up the tall and twisty staircase.

As they neared the top they heard a shuffling noise...

It was Breeze!

"Breeze, Breeze you're here!" Sloop shouted in delight.

Breeze was wrapped up in a warm towel with fish all over her beak. She was in the middle of eating Lighthouse Keeper Kip's sardines!

"Sloop, how did you get here?" Breeze asked.

"I flew over the sea with Mrs Gully. I flew. I FLEW!"

The two friends jumped up and down excitedly.

As the rain continued to pour outside, Sloop, Breeze and Mrs Gully all sat and talked about the big storm adventure.

They talked about how Breeze had got very cold and wet so she came into the lighthouse to keep warm.

They also talked about how brave Sloop had been.

Once the storm had cleared, Sloop, Breeze and Mrs Gully flew back over the sea to where Mr Squawk and Breeze's mum and dad waited for them.

And do you know what? Sloop wasn't scared to fly over the sea any longer, all he had to do now was dive in...

...but that was for another day!